D1342177

THE B

Philip Marlowe is a private detective. He works alone. He thinks for himself, and doesn't trust anybody. When he asks questions, he doesn't expect to get truthful ...rs. When a client gives him a job to do, he tries to ...it honestly, but he knows he might get a bullet in his ...k at any moment.

... Angeles in the 1930s is a city where crime is big ...siness, where people use guns without thinking ...ce. They murder each other for love, for revenge, for money. General Sternwood has four million dollars. He wants Marlowe to get a blackmailer off his back. But is that really what the General wants? He also has two pretty daughters: Vivian, with black hair and long beautiful legs, and Carmen, with golden hair and empty grey eyes. They're lovely, and they're trouble.

Marlowe goes on pushing open doors and asking ...estions, although he knows, from long experience, that he'll only find unpleasant answers.

OXFORD
UNIVERSITY PRESS

Great Clarendon Street, Oxford OX2 6DP

Oxford University Press is a department of the University of Oxford
It furthers the University's objective of excellence in research, scholarship,
and education by publishing worldwide in

Oxford New York

Auckland Bangkok Buenos Aires Cape Town Chennai
Dar es Salaam Delhi Hong Kong Istanbul Karachi Kolkata
Kuala Lumpur Madrid Melbourne Mexico City Mumbai Nairobi
São Paulo Shanghai Taipei Tokyo Toronto

Oxford and Oxford English are registered trade marks of
Oxford University Press in the UK and in certain other countries

ISBN 0 19 423027 9

Original edition © Estate of Raymond Chandler 1939

Fourth impression 2003

First published by Hamish Hamilton 1939
This simplified edition © Oxford University Press 2000

First published in Oxford Bookworms 1991
This second edition published in the Oxford Bookworms Library 2000

Illustrated by Gordon Hendry

Typeset by Wyvern Typesetting Ltd, Bristol
Printed in Spain by Unigraf s.l.

RAYMOND CHANDLER

The Big Sleep

Retold by
Rosalie Kerr

OXFORD UNIVERSITY PRESS

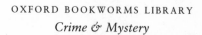

OXFORD BOOKWORMS LIBRARY

Crime & Mystery

The Big Sleep

Stage 4 (1400 headwords)

Series Editor: Jennifer Bassett
Founder Editor: Tricia Hedge
Activities Editors: Jennifer Bassett and Alison Baxter

CONTENTS

1

Marlowe meets the Sternwoods

It was about eleven o'clock in the morning, one day in October. There was no sun, and there were rain-clouds over the distant hills. I was wearing my light blue suit with a dark blue shirt and tie, black socks and shoes. I was a nice, clean, well-dressed private detective. I was about to meet four million dollars.

From the entrance hall where I was waiting I could see a lot of smooth green grass and a white garage. A young chauffeur was cleaning a dark red sports-car. Beyond the garage I could see a large greenhouse. Beyond that there were trees and then the hills.

There was a large picture in the hall, with some old flags above it. The picture was of a man in army uniform. He had hot hard black eyes. Was he General Sternwood's grand-father? The uniform told me that he could not be the General himself, although I knew he was old. I also knew he had two daughters, who were still in their twenties.

While I was studying the picture, a door opened. It was a girl. She was about twenty, small but tough-looking. Her golden hair was cut short, and she looked at me with cold grey eyes. When she smiled, I saw little sharp white teeth. Her face was white, too, and she didn't look healthy.

'Tall, aren't you?' she said.

'I apologize for growing.'

She looked surprised. She was thinking. I could see that thinking was difficult for her.

'Handsome, too,' she said. She bit her lip and half-closed

her eyes. She waited to see what effect that had on me. When I did nothing, she asked, 'Who are you?'

'I'm a detective.'

'What?'

'You heard me.'

'I don't believe you.' She giggled suddenly, and put her thumb in her mouth like a baby. 'You're so tall,' she said.

Then she turned away from me and fell backwards into my arms. I had to catch her to stop her from crashing to the floor. She held on to me and giggled again.

'You're cute,' she giggled. 'I'm cute, too.'

I said nothing. At that moment the butler came in. He didn't look surprised.

He was a tall thin silvery man of about sixty, with expressionless blue eyes. He moved towards us like a much younger man. In a moment the girl had gone.

The butler said, 'The General will see you now, Mr Marlowe.'

'Who was that?' I asked him.

'Miss Carmen Sternwood, sir.'

'I think she should see a doctor. Does she often fall over like that?'

He looked at me coolly, but said nothing.

We went out and walked across the grass. The young chauffeur was cleaning a big black car now. The butler opened a door, and we went into the greenhouse.

It was hot in there, the air thick and wet and the light green. The place was full of plants with heavy flowers and leaves like dead fingers. From a wheelchair in the middle of the greenhouse an old man with black eyes watched us.

*The girl giggled suddenly, and put her thumb
in her mouth like a baby.*

Although it was so hot, he was covered in blankets.

The butler said, 'This is Mr Marlowe, General.'

The old man didn't move or speak. He just looked at me. Then he said, 'Brandy, Norris. Please bring some brandy.'

The butler went and the old man spoke again. He used his weak old voice as carefully as a poor actress uses her last good pair of shoes.

'I used to like champagne with my brandy. Cold champagne. I can't drink now. Please allow me to enjoy watching you drink. Take off your coat, sir. It's too hot in here for a healthy young man. You may smoke. I like the smell of cigarettes.'

I took off my coat and lit a cigarette. The butler brought me brandy and I drank some. The General watched me, with his eyes half-closed.

'Tell me about yourself, Mr Marlowe.'

'There's very little to tell. I'm thirty-three. I used to work for the District Attorney. His chief investigator, Bernie Ohls, told me you wanted to see me. I'm not married. I don't like policemen's wives.'

'Why did you stop working for the District Attorney?'

'I was fired. I don't enjoy taking orders from other people. I like thinking for myself.'

The old man smiled. 'I feel the same myself, sir. I'm glad to hear you say that. What do you know about my family?'

'Your wife is dead. You have two young daughters. They're both pretty and both wild. One of them has been married three times – the last time to a bootlegger called Rusty Regan.'

The General smiled his thin smile.

'I was very fond of Rusty Regan. He was a big red-haired Irishman with sad eyes and a wide smile. He spent hours with me. He was a grand story-teller and a grand drinker. Of course, he was not a suitable husband for my daughter. I'm telling you our family secrets, Mr Marlowe.'

'They'll stay secrets,' I told him. 'What happened to Regan?'

The old man looked at me sadly. 'He went away a month ago. Without saying goodbye. That hurt me. I hope he'll come back. And now someone is blackmailing me again.'

'Again?'

He took a packet of papers from under the blankets. 'Nobody blackmailed me while Rusty was here, you can be sure. But nine or ten months ago I paid a man called Joe Brody five thousand dollars to leave my younger daughter Carmen alone.'

'Ah,' I said.

'What does that mean?'

'Nothing,' I said.

He stared at me. 'Look at this,' he said. 'And have some more brandy.'

I took the packet. The address said: General Guy Sternwood, 3765 Alta Brea Crescent, West Hollywood, California. There was a card inside it with the name Mr Arthur Gwynn Geiger, Specialist Bookseller, but no address. There were also three notes signed by Carmen Sternwood. Each promised to pay Geiger $1,000.

'Any ideas?' the General asked.

'Not yet. Who is Arthur Gwynn Geiger?'

'I don't know.'

The General stared at me. 'Look at this,' he said.
'And have some more brandy.'

'What does Carmen say?'

'I haven't asked her. If I did, she would put her thumb in her mouth and giggle.'

I said, 'I met her. She did that to me. Then she fell over on to me.'

The expression on his face did not change.

'Should I be polite?' I asked. 'Or can I be honest?'

'I think you can decide for yourself, Mr Marlowe.'

'Do the girls spend a lot of time together?'

'I don't think so. Vivian is intelligent but cruel. Carmen is just a selfish child. Neither of them ever worries about the difference between right and wrong. Neither do I.'

'Do they have any money of their own?'

'Vivian has a little. I am generous to them both.'

I drank some brandy. Then I said, 'I can take Geiger off your back, General, if you want me to.' I told him how much money I wanted for the job.

'I see,' he said. 'That seems fair. Very well, Mr Marlowe. The problem is now in your hands.'

'I'll fix Mr Geiger,' I said. 'He'll think a bridge fell on him.'

'I'm sure you will manage excellently. And now you must excuse me. I am tired.'

He touched a bell, stared at me once more, and closed his eyes.

I picked up my coat and went out of that hot greenhouse full of flowers. The cool air of the garden smelled wonderful. The butler was coming towards me.

'Mrs Regan would like to see you, sir. And the General has told me to pay you what is necessary.'

'Told you how?'

He smiled. 'You are, of course, a detective, sir. By the way he rang his bell.'

'Why does Mrs Regan want to see me?'

His blue eyes looked straight into mine.

'She misunderstands the reason for your visit, sir.'

'Who told her about my visit?'

'She saw you enter the greenhouse, sir. I had to tell her who you were.'

'I don't like that,' I said. 'Take me to Mrs Regan's room.'

It was a big white room, too big, too white. Long windows looked out onto the dark hills. It was going to rain soon.

I sat on the edge of a deep soft chair and looked at Mrs Regan. She was lovely. She was trouble. She was lying in a chair with her shoes off, so I stared at her legs. They were long and beautiful. She was tall and strong-looking, with black hair and the hot black Sternwood eyes.

She was drinking, and looked at me coolly over her glass.

'So you're a private detective,' she said. 'I imagined an awful little man.'

I said nothing.

'How did you like Dad?'

'I liked him.'

'He liked Rusty. Do you know who Rusty is?'

'Yes.'

'Rusty was sometimes rough and noisy, but he was never dull. He was a lot of fun for Dad. Why did he just disappear like that? Dad wants you to find him. Isn't that true, Mr Marlowe?'

'Yes and no,' I said.

'Do you think you can find him?'

'I didn't say I was going to try. Why don't you go to the police?'

'Oh, Dad will never bring the police into it.'

She looked at me smoothly, and drank what was left in her glass. Then she rang a bell and a maid came in and filled the glass without looking at me.

Mrs Regan said, 'How will you start?'

'When did Rusty go?'

'Didn't Dad tell you?'

I just smiled at her. She went red and her hot black eyes looked angry. 'Don't play with me,' she said. 'I don't like the way you're behaving.'

'I'm not crazy about you,' I told her. 'I didn't ask to see you, you asked to see me. I don't care if you show your legs and drink whisky for lunch. I don't care if you think I behave badly. You're probably right. But don't try to question me.'

She put her glass down hard. Drops of whisky fell on the white chair.

'Don't talk to me like that,' she said thickly.

I smiled again and lit a cigarette.

'I hate big dark handsome men like you,' she said. 'I just hate them.'

'What are you afraid of, Mrs Regan?' I asked.

Her expression changed. 'You could find Rusty – if Dad wanted you to,' she said.

'When did he go?'

'A month ago. He drove away without a word to anyone. They found his car later.'

'They?'

Suddenly she gave a lovely smile. 'He didn't tell you!'

'I hate big dark handsome men like you,'
Vivian Regan said. 'I just hate them.'

'He told me about Mr Regan. He wanted to see me about something else. Is that what you wanted me to say?'

'I don't care what you say!'

I left her then. In the hall I met Norris.

'You made a mistake,' I said. 'Mrs Regan didn't want to see me.'

'I'm sorry, sir,' he said politely. 'I make many mistakes.'

I stood on the steps and smoked my cigarette. I looked over the garden to the hills. In the distance I could see some old oil-wells. The Sternwoods' money came from those oil-wells. Now they lived in their beautiful house, far from the machines and the smell of the oily water in the sump.

I walked down to the gates and out of the Sternwood garden. The sky was black when I reached my car. I heard thunder in the hills and put the top up on my car.

She had lovely legs. They were a smooth act, General Sternwood and his daughters. 'What do they really want?' I wondered.

2

Mr Geiger's bookstore

Geiger's store was on the north side of the boulevard, near Las Palmas. As I stopped to look in the window, a man in the street gave me a knowing smile. The door closed quietly behind me and I stepped onto a soft blue carpet. There were big comfortable blue armchairs and some expensive-looking books on small tables. In one corner a woman sat at a desk.

She got up slowly and came towards me. She was wearing

a short black dress, which looked good over long legs. She had blonde hair and green eyes. Her fingernails were silver. You don't often buy a book from a girl like that.

'Can I help you?' she asked me.

I asked her for a book. It was a famous book, but she had never heard of it. I tried another name. She didn't know it. She knew as much about books as I knew about painting my fingernails silver.

'I'll have to speak to Mr Geiger,' I told her. 'Is he here?'

'I'm afraid not,' she said. 'He'll be here later.'

'I can wait,' I said. 'I have nothing else to do this afternoon.'

I sat in one of the blue armchairs and smoked a cigarette. Nothing happened. The girl sat at her desk and stared at me. She looked unhappy.

Then the door opened and a tall man with a big nose came in. He hurried past me and put a large packet on the desk. He took something out of his wallet and showed it to the blonde. She touched a button and a door opened. He disappeared through it.

Minutes passed. I smoked another cigarette and the blonde watched me.

The door opened and the tall man came out. He was carrying another large packet. He looked quickly at me as he passed me.

I followed him. Someone who looks like that is easy to follow. When he stopped to cross the street, I let him see me. He walked on quickly and turned left, between two houses surrounded by trees. I stood and waited, as rain began to fall.

Minutes passed. Then he came back and walked straight

past me. He didn't have the packet any more. He was safe now.

I watched him go down the street. Then I went between the houses and found the packet behind a tree. Nobody saw me pick it up.

I went back to the boulevard. I found a phone book and discovered that Geiger lived on Laverne Terrace, a street off Laurel Canyon Boulevard.

Then I went to visit some other stores. In one of them I found a girl who could describe Geiger. She said he was about forty, a fat man with a fat face and a moustache. He dressed fashionably.

I ran back to my car through heavy rain. Then I opened the packet. I knew what was inside it. A heavy book, full of photographs. They made me feel sick. The worst pornography I had ever seen. The book was not new. A lot of people had borrowed it before the man with the big nose. Geiger's store was a library of ugly dirt. To run that business on the boulevard he must be paying someone a lot of protection money. I sat in my car and smoked and thought about it.

3

A dead man disappears

It was raining hard and the rain came through the soft top of my car. I put on my coat and went to buy some whisky. Then I sat in the car and drank whisky while I watched Geiger's store.

Business was good at Geiger's. Very nice cars stopped, and

very nice people walked in and came out with packets in their hands. Not all of them were men.

At four o'clock a white sports-car stopped in front of the store. I saw the fat face and the moustache as he ran in. A tall dark and very good-looking boy came out to park the car.

Another hour passed. It got dark. Just after five the tall boy came out with an umbrella in his hand. He brought the car to the door and then held the umbrella over Geiger as he came out of the store. The boy went back into the store and Geiger drove off.

I followed him. As I hoped, he was going home to Laverne Terrace. It was a narrow street, with houses hidden among wet trees. I saw Geiger drive his car into the garage of a small house. Lights came on. I parked my car outside an empty house.

I had another drink and waited. It was a very quiet street. At about six, lights came towards me through the dark and the rain. The car stopped and a small woman got out and went into Geiger's house. I heard a bell ring and the sound of the door closing. Then it was silent again.

I walked along the street and lit a match to look at the car. It was a dark red sports-car. I had seen it before. At the Sternwood house.

I went back to my car. Everything was quiet. It seemed a nice normal street for a sick criminal like Geiger to live on.

At twenty past seven, there was a sudden bright light from the house. Then I heard a scream. It was a terrible scream, a sound made by someone drunk or mad.

I ran to the front door. As I reached it, I heard three shots. There was a crash and the sound of someone running through the house. A car drove quickly away from the back of the house.

I threw myself against the front door, but that just hurt my shoulder and made me angry, so I kicked in a window.

I stepped through it, into the house. There were two people in the room. Neither of them looked at me, although only one of them was dead.

It was a wide room with a low ceiling. There were Japanese pictures on the walls and a pink Chinese carpet on the floor. There was a lot of silk in that room. The chairs were covered in yellow silk. I saw some silk underclothes on the floor, too. The other thing I noticed was the smell. The sick smell of ether.

Miss Carmen Sternwood was sitting on orange silk. She sat very straight, with her hands on the arms of the chair and her knees together. Her small teeth shone white in her open mouth. Her eyes were wide open, too. They stared crazily at nothing.

She was wearing a pair of long green ear-rings. They were nice ear-rings. She wasn't wearing anything else.

She had a beautiful body, small and finely made, with skin like silk. I looked at her and felt no excitement at all. To me she was never really a woman. She was always just a stupid kid.

Geiger was on his back on the floor, next to a camera. He was wearing a Chinese silk coat. The front of the coat was covered in blood. He was very dead.

I kicked in a window, and stepped through it into the house.

The bright light had come from the camera, the scream from the drugged girl. The three shots were someone else's idea. He had fired those shots and then run to his car and driven away. I could understand why.

I listened to the rain. There was no other sound outside. Then I took off my coat and picked up Miss Sternwood's clothes.

'Now, Carmen,' I said. 'Let's get you dressed.'

She looked at me with empty eyes.

'G–g–go to hell,' she said.

I hit her a couple of times. She didn't mind, but it didn't help at all. I managed to push her into her dress. She giggled and fell into my arms. I sat her in a chair and put her shoes on her feet.

'Let's walk,' I said. 'A nice little walk.'

We walked to Geiger's body. She thought he was cute. She giggled and tried to talk, but no real words came, so I put her in an armchair and she went to sleep. I looked at the camera. It was empty. I didn't like that. I looked over the rest of the house. There was a pretty little bedroom. It smelled like a woman's room, but a man's shirt lay on the bed. It was Mr Geiger's room. I found a notebook with a lot of names in it and put it in my pocket.

I tried to wake Carmen up, but it was impossible, so I carried her to her car. I drove off without lights. It took ten minutes to get to the Sternwood house in Alta Brea Crescent. The smell of ether in the car was horrible. Carmen made loud noises as she breathed in her drugged sleep.

Norris opened the door of the Sternwood house. He said, 'Good evening, sir,' politely, and looked past me at Carmen's car. His eyes met mine silently.

'Is Mrs Regan in?'

'No, sir.'

'The General is asleep, I hope?'

'Yes, sir.'

'Get Mrs Regan's maid. This is a job for a woman. Look in the car and you'll understand.'

'I see,' he said. 'We'll take care of her.'

'I guess you've seen it all before,' I said.

He didn't reply.

'Forget you've seen me,' I told him. 'I'm not here at all.'

He smiled at me as I walked away. It took me half an hour to get back to Geiger's house. I was wet to the skin. The street looked empty and lonely. I got into my car and drank some whisky and smoked a cigarette. Then I went into the house.

There was a new carpet on the floor. It hadn't been there before. Geiger's body had been there. I looked for him. He wasn't in his bedroom, or the kitchen or the bathroom.

I looked carefully at the carpet by the front door. A body had been pulled over it. Dead men are heavy and hard to move.

Who had moved the body? Not the police. Not the killer. I locked the door and went home to eat dinner and change my clothes. After that, I drank too much whisky and studied Geiger's notebook. There were more than four hundred names and addresses in it. A good business. Had he blackmailed his customers? Had one of them killed him?

I went to bed full of whisky and questions.

4

Who killed Owen Taylor?

Next morning was bright and warm. The sun was shining. I drank two cups of coffee and read the newspapers. There was nothing in them about Geiger's death.

The phone rang. It was Bernie Ohls, the District Attorney's chief investigator. He had given my name to General Sternwood.

'How's life?' he began. He sounded happy enough.

'I drank too much last night.'

'Bad boy! Seen General Sternwood yet?'

'Yes.'

'Done anything for him?'

'Too much rain,' I said. It wasn't much of an answer.

'Things seem to happen to the Sternwoods. One of their cars is lying in the sea off Lido Pier.'

I held the phone very close to my ear and stopped breathing.

'A nice new Buick, all full of sea-water. Oh, and I almost forgot. There's a guy in it.'

I breathed out slowly. 'Regan?'

'I don't know. I'm going to see. Want to come with me?'

An hour later I was in his office. Ohls was a gentle-looking man. If you saw him in the street, you would never guess he had killed men.

'It isn't Regan,' he said. 'I checked. Regan's a big guy. This is a young kid.'

We drove out to Lido Pier. The big black car had been pulled out of the water onto a boat. Men in uniform

The big black car had been pulled out of the water onto a boat.

were standing around it.

The driver was still in his seat. He was a thin boy with black hair. A short time ago he had been good-looking. Now his face was bluish-white and there was a wound on one side of his head.

A doctor was working on him. He stared at the dead man's face, felt the wound and looked at his hands.

'His neck is broken,' he said. 'That killed him.'

'What about the wound on his head?' Ohls asked. 'Did he get that when the car crashed?'

'I don't think so,' the doctor said. 'I think he was hit on the head before the car went into the sea.'

'Thanks, Doc,' Ohls said. We got into his car.

'Do you know who he was?' he asked me.

'Yes. He was the Sternwoods' chauffeur. I saw him when I visited the General yesterday.'

'Yeah. His name was Owen Taylor,' Ohls said. 'How do I know? It's a funny thing. He was in trouble with the law a year or two ago. He tried to run off with Carmen Sternwood. The sister ran after them and brought them back. Then she asked us to forget it. It seems Taylor wanted to marry the girl. He'd been in prison before. We told the Sternwoods, but they still gave him his job back. What do you think of that?'

'They're a crazy family,' I said. 'Do they know he's dead?'

'No. I'm going to tell them now.'

'Don't tell General Sternwood. He has enough troubles.'

'Do you mean Regan?'

'No,' I said. 'I'm not looking for Regan. I don't know anything about him.'

Ohls took me to Hollywood and then drove west to Alta

Brea Crescent. I walked along the boulevard to Geiger's store.

The store looked just the same. The same blonde was there, wearing the same black dress.

'Was it . . .?' she said, and stopped. Her silver fingers were shaking with fear. She tried to smile but failed.

'I'm back,' I said. 'Is Mr Geiger here today?'

'I'm . . . I'm afraid not. What . . . what did you want?'

I stood close to her and spoke in a whisper.

'I don't really want to buy anything,' I said. 'I have to be careful. I have something he'll want. Something really hot.'

'Oh, you're in the business,' she said. 'Why don't you come back tomorrow? He'll be here tomorrow.'

'Is he sick? I can go up to his house.'

'No! No. He's out of town. You can't!' She was trembling from head to foot.

Suddenly, the door at the back of the store opened and the tall handsome boy looked out. He was white-faced. He shut the door quickly, but I had seen the boxes and a man packing them. They were moving Geiger's books out.

'Tomorrow, then,' I said to the blonde. 'I'd like to give you my business card, but I'd better not. You understand.'

I went out and looked behind the store. There was a small black truck by the back door. The man was putting boxes of books into it. I went back to the boulevard and found a taxi with a fresh-faced kid at the wheel. I showed him a dollar and asked him to follow the truck.

He looked hard at me. 'You a cop?'

'Private,' I told him.

He smiled. 'Get in, Mac.'

The truck led us across town to Randall Place and stopped

outside a white apartment house. I got out and looked at the names on the mail-boxes in the hall. A Joe Brody lived in Apartment 405. General Sternwood had paid a Joe Brody five thousand dollars to leave Carmen alone and find another little girl to play with. Was it the same Joe Brody?

I went round to the elevator. The truck driver was carrying in the boxes of books.

'Hurry up,' I said. 'Mr Brody's waiting.'

'All right, all right,' he said angrily. 'These books are heavy, you know. Brody can wait.'

I went out into the street again. The taxi took me downtown to my office building.

I had a room and a half on the seventh floor. The half room was my waiting-room. I always left the door open so that if I had a client, he or she could sit and wait for me in comfort.

Today I had a client. She wore a brownish suit, shiny walking shoes and a hat that was no bigger than a one-dollar bill and probably cost fifty dollars.

'So you do come to work,' she said. 'I was beginning to think you stayed in bed all day.'

'Hello, Mrs Regan,' I said. 'Come into my office.'

She stood up and said, 'I'm afraid I wasn't very nice to you yesterday.'

'I wasn't too polite to you,' I said.

We went into my office. She looked at the old carpet, the three chairs and the desk.

'You don't make much money,' she said.

'You can't make big money in this game if you're honest.'

'Oh, are you honest?' she said, and lit a cigarette.

'Terribly honest.'

'What made you become a detective, then?'

'What made you marry a bootlegger?'

'I don't want to argue with you. I've been trying to find you all morning.'

'Because of Owen?'

She looked sad. 'Poor Owen,' she said. 'So you know about that.'

'I know Owen wanted to marry Carmen.'

'Perhaps it wasn't such a bad idea. He was in love with her. We don't see much of that among the people we know.'

'He'd been in prison.'

'That's nothing,' she said. 'He just didn't know the right people. Anyway, I didn't come here to talk about Owen. Can you tell me why my father wanted to see you?'

'No.'

'Was it about Carmen?'

'I can't say.'

She watched me silently for a moment. Then she took something out of her handbag and passed it to me. It was a photograph of Carmen. She was sitting in Geiger's chair, in her ear-rings and nothing else. Her eyes were even crazier than I remembered.

'How much do they want?' I asked.

'Five thousand. They want it tonight. If I don't pay them, they'll go to the newspapers. A woman phoned me. There's something else. She said Carmen was in some other trouble, too, with the police.'

'What kind of trouble?'

'I don't know.'

'Where is Carmen now?'

'She's at home. She was sick last night. She's still in bed.'

'Did she go out last night?'

'No. I did, but she didn't. I went to Las Olindas to play roulette at Eddie Mars's Cypress Club. I lost an awful lot of money.'

'So you like roulette,' I said.

She lit another cigarette. 'Yes, I like roulette. I usually lose. The Sternwoods have lots of money. All it brings us is trouble.'

'Why did Owen have your car last night?'

'Nobody knows. We didn't tell him he could take a car. Do you think . . .?'

'He knew about this photograph? I don't know. Can you get five thousand dollars quickly?'

'I can borrow it from Eddie Mars. He ought to help me.'

'Get the money. You may need it in a hurry. Don't tell the police. You must take care of your father and sister.'

'Can you help?'

'I think I can, but I can't tell you why or how.'

She said suddenly, 'I like you. Do you have anything to drink in this office?'

I took out a bottle of whisky and two glasses. We drank.

'I'll get the money from Eddie,' she said. 'He ought to be nice to me. Rusty Regan ran off with Eddie's wife.'

I said nothing.

'Aren't you interested?' she asked me.

'I'm not looking for Rusty Regan,' I said. 'Now you know what you wanted to know.'

She breathed out slowly. 'Rusty wasn't a crook,' she said. 'He didn't need money. He always carried fifteen thousand

'The Sternwoods have lots of money,' Vivian Regan said.
'All it brings us is trouble.'

dollars with him. He didn't need any cheap blackmail racket.'

She picked up the photograph and went to the door.

'She has a beautiful little body, hasn't she?' she said.

'Yes.'

'You should see mine.'

'Can that be arranged?'

She laughed. 'You're a cold-blooded animal, Marlowe. Or can I call you Phil?'

'OK.'

'You can call me Vivian.'

'Thanks, Mrs Regan.'

'Oh, go to hell, Marlowe,' she said, and walked out.

5

Marlowe meets Eddie Mars

Laverne Terrace was fresh and green after the rain. Everything was quiet.

I drove slowly along the street. I had an idea. I was going to check Geiger's garage.

I never had time to search the garage. As I reached the house, I saw a woman in a green and white coat. It was Carmen Sternwood, of course.

'Hello,' she said in a thin voice. 'What . . . what . . .?' She put her thumb in her mouth.

'Remember me?' I said. 'The tall man.'

I opened the door and pushed her in. The house looked awful in the light of day.

She tried to smile. She wanted to be cute, but her empty

eyes were just stupid. She was a stupid, pretty little girl who was going very, very wrong. Nobody was helping her. I thought, 'These rich people make me sick.'

I sat down and lit a cigarette.

'What do you remember of last night?' I asked her.

'I was sick. I stayed home.'

'Like hell,' I said. 'You were here. In that chair. Before I took you home.'

She turned slowly red.

'You?' she whispered. 'Are you from the police?'

'No. I'm a friend of your father's.'

'What do you want?'

'Who killed him? Did Joe Brody do it?'

I was guessing, but she jumped when she heard the name.

'Yes! Joe did it!'

'Why?'

'I don't know. I hate him!'

'Will you tell the police Joe killed him?' I asked. She looked suddenly afraid.

'I won't tell them about the photos,' I said.

She giggled. It was a sick, crazy sound. It got louder and louder. She couldn't stop laughing. I hit her hard. That stopped her.

'You're a detective,' she said. 'Viv told me.'

'You remember everything,' I said. 'You came to look for the photos, didn't you?'

She tried to smile and look cute.

'The photos have gone,' I said. 'Perhaps Brody took them. Did you tell me the truth about Brody?'

'Yes.'

'Go home now,' I said. 'Don't tell anyone you came here.'

She was at the door when we both heard a car engine. She froze with fear as the door-bell rang. Then someone put a key in the lock. Carmen jumped away from the door as it opened, and a man stepped quietly in.

He was all grey. A grey man in a beautiful grey suit with a grey shirt and two red diamond shapes on his grey tie. I recognized him. It was Eddie Mars. When he saw Carmen, he took off his grey hat politely and smiled smoothly at her.

'Excuse me,' he said. 'Is Mr Geiger here?'

'No,' I said. 'We don't know where he is. We came to get a book.'

Carmen was staring at Mars. I could tell she liked him.

'The girl can go,' he said. 'I want to talk to you. Don't try anything. I've got two good friends outside.'

Carmen made a strange, high sound and ran out of the house.

'There's something wrong around here,' Eddie Mars said. 'I wonder what it is. Don't stand in my way if you want to stay alive.'

'A real tough guy,' I said.

'Only when necessary.'

He wasn't looking at me. He was walking around the room. I looked out of the window. There was a car outside with two men in it.

He found the camera and picked up a couple of books.

'The dirty crook,' he said.

Then he looked down at the floor. His face froze. His hand went under his coat and a gun appeared.

'Blood,' he said. 'A lot of blood. Here, under the carpet.'

'Is there?' I said.

'I'll get the law.'

'OK,' I said. 'Let's do that.'

He didn't like that. 'Who the hell are you?' he asked.

'The name's Marlowe. I'm a private detective. The girl's my client. Geiger was trying to blackmail her.'

'So you just walked into his house?'

'Yeah,' I said. 'Just like you.'

'I own this house,' Mars said. 'Do you have any idea what happened here?'

'Perhaps Geiger killed someone. Perhaps someone killed Geiger. Call the police. They'll be glad to hear from you.'

'What do you mean?'

'I know you, Mr Mars. The Cypress Club at Las Olindas. Gambling for rich people. You've got the law in your pocket. You run protection rackets. Geiger needed protection. Perhaps you did that for him.'

'What racket was Geiger in?'

'Pornography.'

He stared at me. 'Someone killed him,' he said. 'You know something about it. They don't know anything at the store.'

'You missed something,' I said. 'Someone moved his books out of the store today.'

'You notice a lot,' he said. He went to the door and shouted, 'Come in, boys!'

Two men jumped out of the car and ran into the house. They both had guns.

'Search this guy,' Eddie Mars said. 'Get his gun.'

One of the men felt all my pockets carefully.

'Search this guy,' Eddie Mars said. 'Get his gun.'

'He hasn't got a gun,' he said.

'Who is he?'

The man took my wallet out of my pocket and opened it. 'Philip Marlowe. Private detective. Lives at the Hobart Arms on Franklin.'

'OK,' Mars said to the men. 'Now get out.'

'All right, Mr Marlowe,' he said to me. 'Talk.'

'I can't tell you much. I don't know if Geiger is alive or dead. I know the blonde at his store is afraid of something. The guy who's got the books knows what happened. I can guess who that is.'

'Who?'

'I can't tell you. I've got a client.'

'Tell me. I'll pay.'

'I've got nothing to sell,' I said. 'If I discover anything about Geiger, I'll have to inform the police. Now let me go.'

His face changed. He looked mean, fast and tough. He began to lift the gun.

I asked calmly, 'How is Mrs Mars these days? And your big red-haired friend, the Irishman?'

The hand with the gun shook.

'Get out,' he said quietly. 'Just one word of advice. Leave me alone or you'll wish you were dead.'

He watched me as I left. His eyes were like grey ice.

6

Carmen wants her pictures

It was just before five when I arrived at Joe Brody's apartment on Randall Place. There were lights in some windows, and I could hear radios. I took the elevator up to Apartment 405 and rang the bell.

After a long time the door opened. The man behind it was long and thin, with brown eyes in a brown, expressionless face.

I said, 'Geiger?'

He put a cigarette in his mouth. 'What?'

'Geiger. Arthur Gwynn Geiger. The guy who has the books.'

'I don't know anyone of that name,' he said.

'Are you Joe Brody?'

'Yeah.'

I smiled. That made him angry.

'You're Joe Brody,' I said, 'and you don't know Arthur Gwynn Geiger. That's very funny.'

He started to close the door, so I put my foot in it.

'You have Geiger's books, Joe. I have Geiger's list of customers. We ought to talk.'

Something moved in the room behind him.

'Why not?' he said coolly, and I stepped in.

It was a nice room, with good furniture and heavy curtains. I sat down. Brody picked up a large box. I waited.

'I'm listening,' Brody said. 'Cigarette?'

He threw one towards me. As I caught it, he took a gun out of the box.

'Stand up,' he said. 'Move forwards.'

'Well, well,' I said. I didn't move. 'You're the second guy I've met today who thinks a gun in the hand makes him the big white chief. The other guy's name is Eddie Mars. Do you know him, Joe?'

'No.'

'When he knows what you did last night, you'll be finished, Joe.'

He breathed out slowly, still trying to act tough.

'I'll use this gun if I have to,' he said. 'What's your story?'

'Tell your friend to come out from behind the curtain,' I said.

'Come out, Agnes,' he called.

It was the green-eyed blonde from Geiger's store. She looked very unhappy.

'I knew you were trouble!' she said to me, and threw herself into an armchair.

'Start talking,' Brody said.

I lit my cigarette and tasted the smoke.

'There are more than four hundred names on the list. You can make a lot of money out of that many people. Enough to kill for.'

'You're crazy!' the blonde screamed at me.

'Quiet!' Brody told her. She sat there, burning with anger.

'A lovely racket,' Brody said. 'And how did I get this lovely racket?'

'You shot Geiger,' I told him. 'Last night. You took the film out of the camera and ran off. But someone saw you kill him. She'll tell the police what she saw.'

He exploded. 'That goddamned little bitch!'

'Give me the photos, Joe,' I said.

'How much will you pay?'

'Nothing.'

'I need money. Agnes and I have to get away from here.'

'No money,' I said. 'You made your girlfriend phone Mrs Regan and tell her Carmen was in trouble with the police. You were there, Joe. Carmen will say you killed Geiger. Give me the photos and perhaps I can persuade her she made a mistake. Perhaps she drank too much and started imagining things.'

Brody said, 'She hates me. I threw her out. She's too crazy for a simple guy like me. You win. I'll give you the photos.'

He put his gun away. He was putting his hand in his pocket when the door-bell began to ring. It rang and rang. I didn't like it. Who was on the other side of that door? The police? Eddie Mars and his boys?

Brody gave Agnes another gun. 'Watch him,' he said to her. 'Use it if you have to.'

He opened the door and Carmen Sternwood walked in. She was holding a little gun, which she pushed into Brody's face. He went backwards across the room. He was grey with fear.

Agnes turned her gun away from me and towards Carmen. I knocked it out of her hand. For a moment we fought, silently. Then I had the gun. Neither Brody nor Carmen looked at us.

Joe was trying to smile. 'Listen, kid,' he said in a thin, small voice.

Carmen spoke quietly. There was a strange expression on her white face.

'You killed Geiger. I saw you. I want my pictures. Give me my pictures.'

Suddenly, Agnes threw herself at me and bit my hand. I hit her on the head with the gun, and she tried to bite my leg. She was strong.

Brody reached for Carmen's gun, but missed it. There was a bang, and a window broke. He hit Carmen and she fell to the floor. The gun fell, too.

I hit Agnes on the head again, harder this time. Carmen was on her hands and knees, trying to find her gun.

'Don't let her kill me!' Brody screamed.

I began to laugh. I couldn't stop laughing. I picked up Carmen's gun and put it in my pocket.

'Get up, sugar,' I said.

She began to giggle.

I went up to Brody and took his gun. I had all three guns now. I also took the photographs out of his pocket.

'Can I have my pictures?' Carmen said.

'I'll take care of them for you. Go home and wait for me there.'

She put her thumb in her mouth.

'You're cute,' she said. 'Carmen likes you. She likes you a lot.'

She kissed me suddenly, on the mouth.

'Can I have my gun?'

'Later,' I said.

She ran off, smiling like a happy child.

Carmen was on her hands and knees, trying to find her gun.

7

Geiger's friend is a killer

I looked at Carmen's gun. 'To Carmen, love from Owen' was written on it in silver.

'We must agree on a story,' I said to Brody. 'For example, Carmen hasn't been here. That's very important.'

Brody laughed. 'That will cost you something.'

'Perhaps,' I said. 'Don't expect big money, Joe.'

'Why should I help her?'

'OK, Joe,' I said. 'You don't have to be clever. Go to prison if you like. But it could be worse. Two men were murdered last night.'

Agnes began to cry.

Brody said slowly, 'Sit down. Perhaps we ought to talk. What's this about two murders?'

'Tell me the truth,' I said. 'Where were you last night?'

'I was watching Geiger,' he said. 'I knew something about his book racket. I wanted some of the money he was making. I saw two cars at his house. One of them was Vivian Regan's Buick.'

'Do you know what happened to that car?'

'No. Why should I?'

'It fell into the sea with a guy in it.'

That frightened him. He looked sick.

'Listen,' I said. 'Owen Taylor was the Sternwoods' chauffeur. He took the Buick. He was in love with Carmen, and didn't like the games she was playing with Geiger. He shot Geiger and took the film out of the camera. You took the film from him.'

'Yeah,' Brody said, 'but I didn't kill him. I heard the shots and saw him running out of the house. I hit him on the head and took the film, but he got away from me. That's all I know.'

'How did you know Geiger was dead?'

'I was pretty sure,' Brody said. 'He wasn't at the store next day. He didn't answer his phone.'

'Where did you hide Geiger's body?'

'You're mad. I never saw the guy.'

The door-bell rang.

'That goddamned bitch Carmen,' Brody said. 'She's back.'

'I've got her gun,' I said. 'It's OK, Joe.'

He went to the door and opened it. A voice said, 'Brody?' and then there were two shots. Brody crashed to the floor. He didn't move again.

I jumped across the room and ran down the stairs. I saw a man running down the street. As I followed him, bullets hit the wall at my side. He hid behind a row of cars. I took Carmen's gun from my pocket.

As I came up behind him, a police-car drove by. I pushed the gun into his back.

'Me or the cops?' I said.

He turned. He was a tall, very handsome boy, with dark eyes and thick black hair. The boy from Geiger's store.

'Go to hell,' he said.

'Get into my car,' I told him. 'We're going home. Home to Laverne Terrace. You drive.'

He started the car.

'You're a simple guy,' I told him. 'What's your name, boy?'

'Carol Lundgren.'

'You shot the wrong man, Carol. Joe Brody didn't kill your friend Geiger.'

'Go to hell.'

When we got to Geiger's house, I said, 'All right, Carol. Open the door.'

'I don't have a key.'

'You do,' I said. 'You live here. I understand what was going on, Carol.'

I had the gun, but he still tried to hit me. He fought hard, but I was heavier than him, and there was never any question of him winning. When he was unconscious, I put handcuffs on him, and dragged him into the house.

When he opened his eyes, I said, 'Listen to me, brother. You listen hard. You're going to say what we want you to say. Not a word more or less. If you refuse, you'll die in prison.'

'Go to hell.'

I left him to think about things and searched the house. And this time I found Geiger's body – in Carol's room. He lay on the bed in his bloody Chinese coat, cold as ice. Black silk covered the bed, and there was a strange, sweet smell in the room.

I telephoned Ohls at his home.

'This is Marlowe,' I said. 'Did your boys find a gun on Owen Taylor's body this morning? Because if they did, Taylor had fired it three times.'

'How the hell do you know that?' Ohls said quietly.

'Come to 7244 Laverne Terrace, off Laurel Canyon Boulevard. I'll show you where the bullets went.'

8

Marlowe helps the police

Bernie Ohls put Carol Lundgren in his car. I followed in mine. I was glad to see the last of Laverne Terrace.

We drove to the Central Police Station. There was a policeman outside, waiting to guard Carol.

I liked being at the Police Station that night. The police were my friends. They really needed me. I had plenty to give them.

First, I had Carol Lundgren waiting for them in Ohls's car. He had killed Joe Brody. I gave them Carol's gun.

Second, I told them about Owen Taylor, dead in the Buick off Lido Pier. I said he had killed Geiger. This was all news to them.

I told my story well, but I didn't tell them everything. I kept some secrets. Like Carmen's visit to Brody's apartment and Eddie Mars walking into Geiger's house.

They threw me some questions. Why was I so sure Taylor had killed Geiger? Perhaps Brody was the killer?

'No,' I told them. 'Brody was a crook, but not a killer. He wanted Geiger's book racket, but he wasn't clever enough to do two murders – that is, kill Geiger, then put the murder weapon in Taylor's pocket, and then push Taylor into the sea. No, Taylor killed Geiger because he loved Carmen Sternwood, and didn't like what Geiger was doing with her. I think Carol Lundgren hid Geiger's body because he was afraid of the police. Then he changed his mind and put him on the bed. He was very fond of Geiger. Then he went to the store and found someone taking the books to Brody's. He thought Brody had killed Geiger, so he shot him.'

There was silence for a moment. Then Ohls asked, 'Have you told us everything you know?'

'No,' I said.

'Why not?'

'I've given you two killers. I'm a private detective, and I mean private. I take good care of my clients. I don't want anything about the Sternwoods or blackmail to appear in the newspapers.'

'Why should we agree to that?'

'Give me a moment,' I said. I went out to my car and brought in Geiger's book to show them. The policemen looked at the pictures with expressionless faces and shut the book quickly.

'It was obvious what kind of bookstore that really was,' I said. 'But the police allowed it to stay open – for some reason.'

They looked at me with stony eyes and agreed that the Sternwood name could be kept out of the papers.

It was late when I got back to the Hobart Arms. The phone was ringing as I went into my apartment.

'You've been with the cops,' Eddie Mars's voice said. 'Did you keep my name out of it?'

'Why should I?'

'Because you're a sensible guy, who enjoys living.'

'You frighten me,' I said.

He laughed. 'Did you – or did you?'

'I did.'

'Thanks. Who killed Geiger?'

'Read tomorrow's newspapers.'

'Perhaps I can help you,' he said. 'You're looking for Rusty Regan, aren't you?'

'Some people think I am.'

'If you are, come and see me. Any time.'

Before I went to bed, I phoned the Sternwood house. I spoke to Norris.

'Tell Mrs Regan I have the photos,' I said, 'and that everything is all right.'

I read all the newspapers next morning. The story was that Brody had killed Geiger, and then Brody had been killed by Lundgren, who had now been arrested. There was another

I read all the newspapers next morning.

story, too. A chauffeur called Owen Taylor had killed himself. He had been ill and unhappy. The names Sternwood and Marlowe did not appear. It was all very nice and tidy.

9

Marlowe's job is finished – or is it?

I went to the Missing Persons Bureau to talk to Captain Gregory. I told him I was working for General Sternwood.

The Bureau was working for him, too. They were looking for Regan. General Sternwood wanted to find him. The poor old man was very fond of him and had so little to make him happy now. He was afraid that Regan was involved in blackmailing him. I badly wanted to know the truth about that.

Gregory gave me a little information. Regan had disappeared on September 16th. His car was found a few days later, near Mrs Mona Mars's apartment. She had disappeared, too.

Regan had plenty of money. He had been a soldier, and he knew how to use a gun. Had Eddie Mars killed him because he was jealous? I didn't think so. Eddie was a clever businessman, not some jealous boy. He and Mona had separated before she disappeared, and he wasn't trying very hard to find her.

I thought, 'Regan got tired of Vivian and found someone he liked better. It's as simple as that. I wish I had better news for the General.'

One thing interested me. I saw a photograph of Regan. He

had a sad intelligent face. I thought he looked strong, not tough. If I ever saw him, I would recognize him. I wanted to find him before the General died.

As I left the Missing Persons Bureau, I noticed that a grey car was following me.

I went back to my office and wondered what to do next. I wanted a drink, but I didn't want to drink alone. As I was thinking about it, the phone rang.

It was Norris. He told me that General Sternwood was not very well. The newspaper reports had been read to him. My job was finished.

'I didn't kill Geiger, you know,' I told him.

'No, sir.'

'Does the General know about the photographs?'

'Absolutely not, sir.'

'I'll destroy them,' I said.

'The General has asked me to send you a cheque for five hundred dollars.'

'That's generous of him.'

'He wishes to thank you in person when he is feeling a little better, possibly tomorrow.'

'Fine,' I said. 'I'll come and see him.'

That was that. I still didn't want to drink alone, but I opened a bottle anyway.

I thought about what had happened.

'Rusty Regan has left his rich wife for Mona Mars. I don't think Eddie Mars has killed them. He's too clever, and he doesn't need Regan's money. Geiger is dead. Carmen will soon find a new friend. Mrs Regan plays roulette at Eddie Mars's club. She knows him pretty well. Her husband has run off with Eddie's wife. Carol Lundgren will be in prison for a long time. What about me? I failed to report a murder, but I'm OK with the law, and the General is paying me five hundred dollars. If I'm sensible, I'll forget the Sternwoods and have another drink.'

I wasn't sensible. I went to see Eddie Mars.

The Cypress Club had once been a rich man's house by the sea. It still looked like that. I met Eddie Mars in a big room with rose-coloured silk on the walls.

'Have you been here before?' he asked me.

'No. I don't gamble.'

'Your friend Vivian Regan is here tonight. She's playing roulette. She's winning, too.'

He gave me a drink.

'I like the way you work,' he said. 'How much do I owe you?'

'For what? I don't want money, Eddie. I've been paid. I don't earn a lot, but I'm happy with it. I want information from you. You didn't kill Regan, did you?'

He laughed. 'You can't believe I did.'

'No. I don't believe you did.'

'Why are you interested? Vivian doesn't care about him.'

'Her father does. I think he's afraid Regan was involved in a blackmail racket with Geiger.'

'No,' Mars said. 'Geiger was on his own. You know as much as I do about that business.'

I finished my drink. 'OK, Eddie,' I said. 'I'm going to visit your club now.'

'I couldn't tell you much,' he said. 'My friend Gregory at the Missing Persons Bureau could tell you as much. Perhaps one day I'll be able to help you more.'

'One thing,' I said. 'I've been followed by someone in a grey Plymouth. Do you know anything about that?'

'Hell, no,' he said. He looked really surprised, and a little worried. I wondered why.

10

Marlowe has woman trouble

Eddie Mars's club was a beautiful place. It was full of beautiful people, and Vivian Regan, with her black hair and her low-cut green dress, was at the centre of them. There was music and dancing, but those things didn't interest the beautiful people. They were there to play roulette.

I got a drink from the bar and went to watch Vivian Regan gambling. Everyone was watching her. Her face was white as she cried, 'One more play! Everything on the red!' She had sixteen thousand dollars in front of her. A lot of money to lose.

The wheel turned. The money lay on the red diamond. The little white ball flew around the wheel. Silently, the beautiful people watched. Vivian opened her mouth slowly, and her teeth caught the light like little sharp knives. The wheel turned more and more slowly. The ball stopped moving.

'The red wins.'

Vivian put her head back and laughed. She started to pick up the thousand-dollar bills.

I picked up my hat and walked out of the club. It was dark and foggy outside. Waves crashed onto rocks not far from where I stood. I heard a woman's quick footsteps coming towards me, but I couldn't see her.

Vivian Regan had sixteen thousand dollars in front of her.
A lot of money to lose.

Suddenly the footsteps stopped. A man's voice said, 'Give me the money. Quick, or I'll use this gun.'

I heard her answer, 'Here, take it,' in a low, tired voice, and the sound of the man running off.

'Mrs Regan,' I called softly.

'Marlowe. What are you doing here?'

'Eddie Mars wanted to see me.'

'Why?'

'He thought I was looking for the man who ran off with his wife,' I said.

'Were you?'

'No. Would you like me to find him?'

'No. Although he was my husband.' Suddenly she looked older, harder.

'Where's your car?' I asked her. 'You shouldn't walk around alone at night.'

She laughed. 'I came with a friend. He's drunk. Let's take your car, Marlowe. I want a drink. Will you drink with me?'

We drank black coffee and whisky in a little bar in Las Olindas. I watched Vivian's face. She looked beautiful and wild.

'What do you know about Eddie Mars?' I asked her. 'What does he know about you? Why does he let you play roulette at his club and then take the money back if you win?'

She laughed. 'Let's talk about something else.'

'OK. How's the General today?'

'Not well. Why are you questioning me?'

'How much does he know?'

'Everything, I expect. The District Attorney came to see him. Did you burn the pictures?' she asked.

'Of course.'

'I care a lot about Carmen,' she said. 'And about Dad, too. I don't want him to hate his own children.'

She drank some coffee and lit a cigarette.

'You shoot people,' she said quietly. 'You kill.'

'Me? How?'

'I knew it as soon as I saw you. The police and the newspapers kept it quiet. I know what you've done. Let's go.'

We drove along the coast road. Fog rose from the sea. The world was wet and empty.

'Drive down to the water,' she said. 'I want to look at the sea.'

I parked the car and turned the lights off. Waves crashed onto the beach.

'Kiss me,' she said quietly.

I put my arms around her. Her soft hair touched my face. I lifted her face to mine and kissed her mouth. Her lips opened and she began to tremble.

'Killer,' she said softly.

I kissed her again, harder this time. After a long time she said, 'Where do you live?'

'Hobart Arms, near Kenmore. Want to go there?'

'Yes.'

'What's between you and Eddie Mars?'

She pulled away from me violently.

'So that's the way it is,' she said.

'That's the way it is. Your father didn't hire me to kiss you.'

'You son of a bitch,' she said calmly.

'What's between you and Eddie Mars?'

'If you say that again, I'll scream.'

'Then scream. I told you I was a detective. I work at it, I don't play.'

'I hate you,' she said. 'Drive me home.'

'I enjoyed kissing you,' I said.

She didn't speak to me again. I drove her to Alta Brea Crescent. Then I went home.

There was something wrong with my apartment. I didn't know what it was, but there was something. I went slowly into the bedroom and turned on the light.

Someone giggled. Carmen Sternwood was lying in my bed.

'Cute, aren't I?' she said. 'I've got no clothes on.'

'Nice,' I said. 'The trouble is, I've seen it all before. I saw you at Mr Geiger's house. Remember?'

She giggled.

'Listen,' I said. 'I'm tired. Thanks for what you're offering. It's generous of you, but I'm trying to help your father, not kill him. Please go home, Carmen.'

She stopped giggling. Her mouth opened like a black hole in her white face, and inhuman sounds began to come from it.

Suddenly I had to get her out. I had no family, but that room held books and pictures I loved, letters and good times I remembered. That girl destroyed everything just by being there.

I said carefully, 'You have three minutes to get out.'

When she had gone, I opened the window and the cold night air blew in. I drank some whisky. Then I looked at my bed. The shape and smell of her body were still there. Roughly, violently, I pulled the bed to pieces.

11

'I know where Mona Mars is'

It was raining in the morning. I woke up with an empty feeling. I had two cups of black coffee for breakfast.

The grey Plymouth followed me as I drove to my office, and a small, bright-eyed man followed me up the stairs.

'I'm Harry Jones,' he said. 'Agnes sent me. I've got something to sell. It'll cost you two hundred dollars.'

'Agnes! She's a big girl for a little man like you,' I said.

'Don't talk like that about Agnes. She's my girl now, and I don't allow any guy to talk about her like that.'

I stared at him. 'OK,' I said. 'What are you selling?'

'Information about Rusty Regan.'

'I'm not looking for him.'

'Do you want it or not?'

'Go on. I'm listening.'

'Eddie Mars had Regan killed,' he said calmly.

'I don't believe you. You can go now.'

'You listen to me,' he said sharply. 'I came here to tell you something, and I'm going to tell you. Rusty Regan was in love with a singer called Mona Grant. She married Eddie Mars. You know who Rusty married. She had a rich dad, but Rusty didn't want the money. He still wanted Mona. He left his wife. In the middle of September he disappeared. So did Mona Mars. Eddie didn't look too unhappy about that.'

'I know all this,' I said. 'Everyone knows this.'

'Listen to me. There's plenty you don't know.' He went on, 'My old friend Joe Brody thought he could get some money

'I'm Harry Jones,' he said. 'Agnes sent me.
I've got something to sell.'

from the Sternwoods and from Eddie Mars. Do you know Lash Canino?'

'No.'

'He's tough,' Harry said. 'He does jobs for Eddie Mars. He's a killer. Joe followed him one day and saw him talking to Regan's wife.'

'What does Canino look like?' I asked.

'Short, heavy, has brown hair, brown eyes. He wears brown clothes, drives a brown car. Everything brown for Mr Canino.'

'Go on with the story.'

'I know where Eddie's wife is,' he said. 'She never ran off with Regan. She's hiding near L.A. Will you pay me two hundred dollars to tell you where?'

'Where is she?' I was interested.

'Agnes knows. Agnes found her. She'll tell you when you give her the money.'

He took one of my cigarettes and lit it. He looked a very small man in a world of big tough guys.

'I'll pay,' I said. 'But can't you tell me? Why do I have to talk to Agnes?'

'I promised her,' he said quietly. 'Come to Walgreen's office in the Fulwider Building on Santa Monica at seven tonight.'

After he had gone, I got the two hundred dollars from the bank. I thought about Harry Jones and his story. Why hadn't Captain Gregory found Mona Mars? Had he tried to find her?

Nobody came to see me that day. Nobody phoned. It just went on raining.

12

The small man sleeps the big sleep

At seven o'clock I was in the elevator of the Fulwider Building. I stepped out and started looking for Walgreen's office. Then I heard Harry Jones's voice.

'Canino?' he said. 'Yeah, I know who you are.'

I froze. Another voice spoke. It was a slow, heavy sound. 'I thought you'd know my name,' it said smoothly.

There was an open door beside me. I slid behind it and listened.

The smooth voice went on, 'You went to a detective. That was a mistake. Eddie doesn't like it. Why did you do it?'

'Because of Agnes. She was Joe Brody's girl. She needs money. She's got some information about the Sternwoods that Marlowe wants. He'll pay her for it.'

'Where is Agnes?'

'I won't tell you,' Harry Jones said. 'She's my girl now. You can't speak to her.'

'Oh, can't I?' Canino said. 'Do you see this, little man?' I knew he had taken out a gun. 'Where is she?'

'You win,' Harry Jones said. 'Apartment 301, 28 Court Street. She'll tell you what she knows.'

'That's sensible of you,' Canino said. 'Let's have a drink and then we'll go together to see her.' I heard him take out glasses and open a bottle.

'Good health,' Canino said.

Harry Jones said softly, 'Success.'

I heard a short sharp cry. Then a crash.

Canino said, 'You sick after just one drink, friend?'

Harry didn't reply.

'Goodbye, little man,' Canino said. A door opened and he walked slowly away.

I found Harry Jones sitting in a chair. His eyes were open, his face bluish, frozen in a kind of smile. I smelled whisky, but there was another smell, too. I recognized it. Cyanide.

The first thing I did was phone 28 Court Street. There was no girl called Agnes at Apartment 301.

'You were a good friend to that girl, Harry,' I said. 'You died like a dog, but you're no dog to me, Harry Jones.'

I was leaving when the phone rang. I listened to it for a moment. Then I picked it up and said, 'Yeah?'

'Is Harry there?'

'Not just now, Agnes.'

'Who's that?'

'Marlowe,' I said. 'The guy that's trouble for you.'

'Where's Harry?'

'He ran away,' I told her. 'Canino was after him. Harry wanted to sell me some information. I've got two hundred dollars for him, but now he's gone. You can tell me what I need to know. Do you want the money?'

'I want it,' she said. 'I want it badly.'

'Meet me by the Bullocks Building on Wilshire in half an hour.'

I left the dead man sitting there, and walked out into the rain.

Half an hour later I sat with Agnes in the grey Plymouth as she told me her story.

'Joe and I were out driving the Sunday before last. We passed a brown car and I saw the girl who was driving it. She

I sat with Agnes in the grey Plymouth as she told me her story.

was a blonde. Eddie Mars's wife. Canino was with her. Joe followed the car. They're out east of Realito, in the hills. There's a small garage, which is owned by a man called Art Huck, and a house. She's in that house.'

'Are you sure it's her?'

'Sure. If you ever see her, you won't forget her.'

I gave her the money. Three men were dead, Geiger, Brody and Harry Jones, and blonde Agnes drove off with two hundred dollars, away from all the trouble. Some girls are like that.

I drove out of town, through Pasadena and then through miles of orange trees. The road was wet and dark. It went up into the hills. A sign said Realito.

Suddenly, there was something wrong with my car. I couldn't control it any more. It was built for the city, not these rough country roads. I had to stop. I could see the lights of a building. Was it Art Huck's garage? Was I really this close to Mona Mars?

I put a gun in my pocket and walked along the road. Art Huck's name was on the garage wall. I started to laugh. Then I thought of Harry Jones and I stopped laughing.

I banged on the door.

'We're closed,' a rough voice said. 'Go back to Realito.'

'I can't,' I shouted back. 'My car's broken down. I can't move it.'

Another voice, a smooth voice, said, 'Open the door, Art.'

I went into the garage. It smelled of hot paint. Art Huck was a tall thin man. The other man had a short, thick, strong body. He had a cool face and dark eyes. His brown coat and brown hat were wet with rain.

'Where are you from?' he asked me.

'Santa Rosa. I'm going to L.A., or trying to.'

'It's a rough night,' he said. 'Go and fix the car, Art.'

I was alone with Canino.

'Have a drink,' he said. 'Going to L.A. on business?'

I remembered Harry Jones as I drank. I didn't want to talk to Canino. I wanted to go.

Art Huck came in from the rain.

'It'll take some time for me to fix that car,' he said. 'I can't do it tonight.'

I never knew which of them hit me first. I saw nothing strange, no sign from one man to the other, but one of them hit me. White light exploded inside my head, and then I fell, down and down, into the middle of the black night.

13

Mona Mars helps Marlowe to escape

There was a woman, and she was sitting near a light. The light made her blonde hair shine like silver. She wore a green dress. She was smoking a cigarette, and she had a glass in her hand.

I moved my head carefully. It hurt. I was tied up with rope, and there were handcuffs on my wrists.

'Hello,' I said.

The woman looked at me. Her eyes were the cool blue of mountain lakes.

'How do you feel, Mr Marlowe?' Her voice was silvery, like her hair.

'I feel wonderful,' I said. 'Would you mind moving the light? It's a little too bright for me.'

She moved it.

'I don't think you're very dangerous,' she said. She was tall, but not too tall, thin, but not bony.

'Where are the boys?' I asked her.

'They had to go out.'

'You mean they left you alone? I thought you were a prisoner here.'

She looked amused. 'Why did you think that?'

'I know who you are,' I said.

'Then you're in big trouble,' Mona Mars said. 'I hate killing.'

'You hate killing? You – Eddie Mars's wife!'

She looked angry.

'Why did you come here? Eddie hasn't done anything to you. I told you, I'm not a prisoner here. I want to be here, to help my husband. I want the police to think I ran off with Rusty Regan. They mustn't think Eddie killed him.'

'Your Eddie,' I told her, 'is into every kind of racket. Gambling, pornography, blackmail, protection—'

'He isn't a killer.'

'He has Canino to kill for him,' I said. 'Canino killed a man tonight. I almost saw it. He was a nice, harmless little guy.'

'I love Eddie,' she said. 'He's good to me.'

'If he's so good,' I said, 'I'd like to talk to him without Canino. Canino will knock out my teeth and then shoot me because I can't say "Thanks".'

She stared at me. Then she went out of the room and came back with a knife in her hand. She cut my ropes.

'I can't do anything about the handcuffs,' she said. 'Canino has the key. Go quickly.'

'Come with me,' I said. 'You can't stay here.'

'I'm not afraid. And I still love Eddie. I don't care what he's done.'

'You're coming with me. How long do you think you'll live, when Canino comes back and finds me gone?'

'No! Get out! I know you think Eddie killed Rusty Regan. I don't believe it! You'll find Rusty some day, alive and well!'

'OK,' I said. 'I'm going. But first kiss me, Mrs Mars.'

She put her hands up to my face and kissed me, but her lips were as cold as ice.

It was dark and wet outside. I had reached my car and picked up a gun before I heard the sounds of Canino's car coming back. He left it unlocked and went into the house. I was tired and cold and I was wearing handcuffs. I had to be clever.

I got into Canino's car and started the engine. Then I hid behind the car.

A window opened and three bullets tore into the car. Broken glass fell all around me. I screamed. It was a terrible scream, full of pain. Canino liked it. He liked it a lot. He laughed loudly.

The door opened and Mona Mars was pushed into the rain.

'I can't see him,' she said. Then she stopped and screamed, 'He's there! In your car!'

Canino knocked her out of his way as he ran forwards. Three more shots banged into the car.

I said, 'Have you finished?'

As he turned towards my voice, I shot him. I shot him four

As he turned towards my voice, I shot him.

times, in the chest. The gun jumped out of his hand, and he fell on his face without a sound.

I kicked the gun away from his body and picked it up. Without a word, Mona Mars took the key from the dead man and unlocked my handcuffs.

14

'Find him for me, Marlowe'

It was another day, and the sun was shining again.

Captain Gregory of the Missing Persons Bureau stared heavily at me.

'I guess you think it was my job to find Mona Mars,' he said.

'That's a fair guess.'

'Perhaps I knew where she was,' he said. 'Perhaps Eddie pays me to keep quiet.'

'I don't really believe that,' I said.

'I'm honest,' he told me. 'I want you to believe that. I'd like to see rich crooks like Eddie Mars in prison, but it isn't easy to catch the big fish.'

He waited for a moment before he said, 'I don't think he killed Rusty Regan. I talked to Mars last night. He told me he employed Canino as a bodyguard. He didn't know Jones or Brody. He knew Geiger, of course, but he says he didn't know anything about his racket. I guess you know all this.'

'Yes,' I said.

'What happened to Mrs Mars?'

'I don't know. The police let her go.'

'They say she's a nice girl.'

'She is a nice girl,' I said.

'One more thing, Marlowe,' Gregory said. 'If you want to help the Sternwoods, leave them alone. Don't try to find Regan.'

'Perhaps you're right, Captain,' I said. I wondered what he knew.

I drove home. I needed to sleep, but I couldn't sleep. I had a drink and remembered how I had driven through the rain with Mona Mars beside me in the car, to tell the police that I had killed Canino. I had taken them to the Fulwider Building, where Harry Jones still sat dead in a chair.

I watched the sun moving down my bedroom wall. Then the phone rang. It was Norris. The General wanted to see me.

It was five days since I had first visited the Sternwood house. It felt like a year.

General Sternwood was in bed. He looked grey and bloodless, but his black eyes were still full of fight.

He looked at me silently for a long time before he said, 'I didn't ask you to look for Rusty Regan.'

'You wanted me to find him,' I said.

'I didn't ask you to. I paid you to do something else.'

'General Sternwood,' I said. 'If you want me to, I'll give you back your money. I know you were afraid Regan was involved in the blackmail business.'

He started to speak, but I went on, 'You don't care about money. You don't even care about your daughters. But you want to know the truth about Regan. You want to know because you really liked him.'

He was silent. Then he said, 'You talk too much, Mr Marlowe. Are you still trying to find him?'

'No,' I said. 'Not now.'

He smiled. 'Don't stop searching for him,' he said. 'I'll pay you another thousand dollars to find him. I want to know if he's all right. If he needs money, I'll give him some. Is that clear?'

'Yes, General.'

He was too tired to speak for a while.

Then he said, 'I'm so fond of that boy. Find him for me, Marlowe. Just find him.'

As I left the house, I saw Carmen in the garden. She was sitting on a step, looking small and lonely.

'Bored?' I asked her.

She smiled and whispered, 'Are you still angry with me?'

'I thought you were angry with me.'

She put her thumb in her mouth and giggled, 'No, I'm not.'

'I've got your gun,' I said. 'I've cleaned it for you. Use it carefully, Carmen.'

'Yes,' she said, and took it from me.

Then she said, 'Teach me how to shoot. I'd like that.'

'Where? You can't start shooting here.'

'I know where,' she said in a secret voice. 'Down by the old oil-wells.'

'All right.'

She smiled like a child as we drove through the empty, sunny morning. It took only a few minutes to reach the wells. This was where the Sternwood fortune had been made. Now it was disused, full of rubbish. There was a bad smell from the oily sump.

I gave Carmen her gun. Then I picked up an old bottle.

'Take it easy,' I said. 'There are five bullets in the gun. I'll put this bottle on the wheel over there. See? Don't shoot until I get back to you.'

'OK,' she giggled.

I walked around the sump and put the bottle in the middle of the wheel. Then I walked back towards her. When I was a few metres from her, at the edge of the sump, she showed me her sharp little teeth and pointed the gun at me.

I stopped. The smelly, oily sump water was just at my back.

'Stand there, you son of a bitch,' she said. Her face was white. She looked old, sick, not quite human.

I laughed at her. I walked towards her and she fired the gun at me. I stopped and laughed again. She fired four more shots.

'You're really cute, Carmen,' I said.

Her hand began to shake violently. The gun fell to the ground. Then her mouth shook and her eyes turned upwards in her head. I caught her as she fell.

I laughed at her. I walked towards her and she fired the gun at me.

15

Sleeping the big sleep

Once again I was in Vivian Regan's white room. I waited for a long time before she came in.

She was wearing white silk, and her fingernails were blood red.

'How could you do it?' she said quietly. 'You killed a man last night. Never mind how I know that. Then you came here and frightened my sister out of her mind.'

I said nothing. She lit a cigarette and blew grey smoke at me.

'What did you do to Carmen?' she asked.

'Nothing. I went to speak to her because I had her gun. She took it to Brody's place the night he was killed. I had to take it away from her. Perhaps you didn't know that.'

She was silent.

'She wanted me to teach her how to shoot,' I said. 'We went down to the old oil-wells. You know the place. I put a bottle on a wheel for her to shoot at. She had a fit and became unconscious. She's a very sick girl, Mrs Regan.'

'Yes,' she said in a small voice. 'I know. Was that all you wanted to tell me?'

'I guess you won't tell me what hold Eddie Mars has over you?'

'He hasn't got a hold over me.'

'Never mind. I think I understand everything that's been happening here. Geiger, Brody, Mars, Canino. It all ties together.'

'I'm afraid I don't understand what you mean.'

'I'll tell you. Geiger was using Carmen to blackmail your father, but Eddie Mars was behind Geiger, just using him. Your father didn't pay Geiger, which showed that he wasn't frightened of him. Eddie wanted to know that. He had a hold over you, and wanted to know if he had it over the General, too. If he had, it would bring him a lot of money very quickly. If not, he would have to wait until you got your half of the family fortune. Owen Taylor killed Geiger, because Owen loved your sister. Eddie didn't care. Only you, Eddie and Mr tough guy Canino knew what game Eddie was playing. Rusty Regan disappeared, and Eddie hid his wife out at Realito so that people would think Rusty had run off with Mona. Eddie knew what had really happened to Rusty, but he didn't want the police to know. Is this very boring for you to listen to?'

'I'm tired of it,' she said. 'So tired.'

'I'm sorry. Your father offered me a thousand dollars this morning to find Regan. That's a lot of money to me, but I can't do it.'

'Why not?' Suddenly she looked frightened.

'I'll tell you,' I said.

For a moment I thought she was going to scream. Then she remembered she was a Sternwood, and she gave me a cool smile.

I took out Carmen's gun and put it very carefully on her knee. She didn't move.

'It's empty,' I said. 'But it had five bullets in it. She fired them all at me. I expected her to, so I put blanks in it. Cute, isn't she?'

'You're crazy,' she said thickly. 'A terrible, crazy man. And you can't prove a thing.'

'Oh, I don't want to prove she shot at me,' I said. 'I'm thinking of the time she used real bullets. The time she killed Regan. He took her down to the old oil-wells, too. She shot him for the same reason she tried to shoot me.'

The gun fell off her knee onto the floor, and she hid her face in her hands.

'Do you want to know why she shot at me? Because she got into my bed and I threw her out of it. I guess Regan did the same to her. But nobody can do that to Carmen.'

'I suppose you want money,' she whispered. 'You son of a bitch.'

'Oh yes,' I said. 'Money talks, doesn't it, Mrs Regan? The only money I'll take is what your father pays me. That poor, sick old man who wants to believe that, although they're a bit wild, his two little girls are not crooks or killers. The old man who wants to find his friend Rusty before he dies. You can call me a son of a bitch. Your sister has called me worse things. I don't care.'

She was silent, a woman made of stone.

'Take her away,' I said. 'Put her somewhere where they'll watch her and keep her away from guns and knives and drinks. Do it fast.'

She turned away from me and looked out of the window.

'He's in the sump,' she said. 'It's true. Everything you said. She told me what she'd done. Just like a child. She's sick, I know. I went to Eddie for help. If Dad knew, he would tell the police. And then he would die. And that's what he would think about before he died. I had to keep it from him.'

'So you let her go free,' I said.

'I'll take her away now, I promise. Eddie . . .'

'Forget Eddie. I'll take care of him.'

'He'll try to kill you.'

'Yeah,' I said. 'His tough guy Canino couldn't. Does Norris know?'

'He'll never tell anyone,' she said.

'I thought he knew.'

I went out quickly. I saw nobody. In the garden I felt there were ghosts watching me. I drove away.

'When you are dead, you have peace,' I thought, 'not before. When you are sleeping the big sleep, you don't care if you are in the oily sump or a great church. Life's horrors don't worry you any more. And the General doesn't have to know. He can lie quietly in his bed, waiting. And in a little while he too, like Rusty Regan, will sleep the big sleep.'

I went into a bar and had a couple of drinks. They didn't make me feel good. They made me think about silver-haired Mona Mars, and I never saw her again.

GLOSSARY

bitch/son of a bitch *(slang)* a bad name to call a woman/man (a bitch is a female dog)

blackmail *(v)* to order somebody to give you money, so that you will not talk about information that could harm him

blank (blank cartridge) blanks in a gun make a loud noise when the gun is fired, but no bullets come out

blonde *(n* and *adj)* a woman with yellow or golden hair

bootlegger someone who makes or sells alcohol in a country where drinking alcohol is against the law (as it was in the USA from 1920 to 1933)

boulevard a wide city street, often with trees on each side

brandy a strong alcoholic drink

butler the chief male servant in a rich person's house

champagne an expensive, bubbly white wine from France

chauffeur a person who is employed to drive a rich person's car

client somebody who buys help or advice from professional people (e.g. lawyers, private detectives)

cop *(informal)* a police officer

crook *(informal)* a dishonest person or a criminal

cute sweet, pretty

cyanide a deadly poison

District Attorney a lawyer in the USA who works for the state

dollar bill a dollar bank note (paper money)

drugged unconscious or behaving strangely as a result of taking drugs

elevator *(American)* a lift

ether a drug which makes you unconscious if you breathe it in

fingernail the hard covering at the end of a finger

fire *(v)* (1) to take an employee's job away; (2) to shoot a bullet from a gun

fit *(n)* a sudden attack of illness, which causes unconsciousness and violent movements of the body

footstep the sound made by feet walking or running

gambling playing games of chance, e.g. roulette, for money

general *(n)* a very important army officer

giggle *(v)* to laugh in a silly, excited, and sometimes childish way

goddamned *(adj, American)* a swearword used to show anger

greenhouse a building with glass walls and roof, used for growing plants which need a warm place

guy *(informal)* a man

handcuffs a pair of metal rings joined together, which are put around a prisoner's wrists

hell/go to hell *(informal)* an angry way of saying 'go away'

hold *(n)* some power which one person has over another

horrible very unpleasant, causing horror

investigator a person who finds out about crimes or mysteries; a detective

kid *(n, informal)* a child or young person

maid a female servant

mail-box *(American)* a box by a door or in an apartment building where people's letters are left by the postman

Missing Persons Bureau an office in the US which tries to find people who have disappeared

oil-well a place where oil is taken out of the ground

pier a platform of wood or metal, built out into the sea

pornography disgusting pictures or descriptions of sexual acts, made in order to cause sexual excitement

protection paying money to criminals so that your business, house, etc., will not be attacked by them

racket a dishonest or unlawful way of making money

roulette a gambling game in which a small ball falls into one of many possible places on a turning wheel

shot *(n)*   the action of firing a bullet from a gun, or the noise it makes

silk   a very soft and expensive natural material, used for clothes, etc.

store *(American)*   a shop

sump   a container which collects unwanted oil, water, etc.

truck   a lorry; a large strong motor vehicle for carrying goods, etc.

The Big Sleep

ACTIVITIES

ACTIVITIES

Before Reading

1 **Read the back cover and the story introduction on the first page of the book. How much do you know now about this story? Choose the best words to complete this passage.**

Philip Marlowe was a *detective / policeman*, who lived in *New York / Los Angeles*. In the *1970s / 1930s* this was a *quiet / tough* city, where people could make a lot of money from *crime / business*. Marlowe saw the *dark / good* side of Los Angeles, and he knew that the answers to his questions would usually be *lies / the truth*.

General Sternwood was a very *poor / rich* man, but he was *old / young* and *sick / healthy*, and he was having problems with a *blackmailer / client*. His two *sisters / daughters* were both *ugly / beautiful* and *sensible / wild*. They were in *trouble / love*, too, and it was all much *better / worse* than the General knew. Could Marlowe do anything to help the Sternwoods?

2 **Can you guess what happens in this story? Choose Y (yes), N (no), or P (perhaps) for each sentence.**

1 General Sternwood is being blackmailed because of something one of his daughters has done. Y/N/P
2 The blackmailer is caught and sent to prison. Y/N/P
3 One of the General's daughters is murdered. Y/N/P
4 One of the Sternwoods kills someone. Y/N/P
5 Marlowe falls in love with one of the girls. Y/N/P

ACTIVITIES

While Reading

Read Chapters 1 to 4. Match these halves of sentences, and complete them with the right names.

Philip Marlowe   *General Sternwood*   *Owen Taylor*
Vivian Regan   *Carmen Sternwood*   *Rusty Regan*
Bernie Ohls   *Arthur Gwynn Geiger*

1 _____, a rich old man, wanted Marlowe to help him . . .

2 _____, an Irish bootlegger, was Vivian's husband, . . .

3 _____, the District Attorney's chief investigator, . . .

4 _____, who was found dead in the sea inside a Buick, . . .

5 _____ discovered that Geiger's business was pornography,...

6 _____ went to see Marlowe at his office . . .

7 _____ was killed while he was taking photographs of Carmen, . . .

8 _____, drugged and wearing only a pair of ear-rings, . . .

9 was at Geiger's house when he was murdered.

10 because someone was blackmailing him.

11 who had disappeared suddenly, without saying goodbye.

12 was in love with Carmen, and wanted to marry her.

13 sent Marlowe to see General Sternwood.

14 because she was worried about her father and sister.

15 and then his body disappeared.

16 and then went to his house and found him dead.

Before you read Chapter 5, which of these ideas do you agree with, and which do you disagree with? Why?

1 Marlowe will soon try to talk to Joe Brody.
2 The same person killed Geiger and Owen Taylor.
3 Rusty Regan will soon come back.
4 Carmen will try to find the photos Geiger took of her.

Read Chapters 5 to 8, and answer these questions.

1 Why did Carmen go back to Geiger's house?
2 What did Marlowe refuse to tell Eddie Mars?
3 Who was hiding in Joe Brody's apartment?
4 Why did Carmen accuse Joe Brody of killing Geiger?
5 What did Joe take from Owen Taylor?
6 Why did Carol Lundgren shoot Joe Brody?
7 Where did Marlowe find Geiger's body?
8 Who killed Geiger, and why?
9 Why did the police agree to keep the Sternwood name out of the papers?
10 What did the newspapers say about Owen Taylor's death?

Before you read Chapter 9, think about these possibilities. Which do you think are more probable? Why?

1 Marlowe's job for General Sternwood is now finished.
2 Marlowe decides to look for Rusty Regan.
3 Regan is involved in blackmailing General Sternwood.
4 Vivian Regan wants to stop Marlowe finding Rusty.
5 Eddie Mars knows what has happened to Rusty.

Read Chapters 9 to 12. Who said this and to whom? Where were they, and what was happening at the time?

1 'I like the way you work. How much do I owe you?'
2 'What's between you and Eddie Mars?'
3 'Cute, aren't I? I've got no clothes on.'
4 'I know where Eddie's wife is.'
5 'You sick after just one drink, friend?'
6 'If you ever see her, you won't forget her.'
7 'It'll take some time for me to fix that car. I can't do it tonight.'

Before you read Chapter 13, can you guess the answers to these questions? Choose from these names.

Lash Canino / Art Huck / Mona Mars / Eddie Mars / Marlowe
1 Who will help Marlowe?
2 Who will kill someone?
3 Who will be killed?

Read Chapters 13 to 15. What do we learn in these chapters about the following?

1 How Mona Mars felt about her husband
2 What happened to Rusty Regan
3 Carmen Sternwood's health
4 The hold Eddie had over Vivian
5 What Norris knew
6 Who General Sternwood cared about

ACTIVITIES

After Reading

1 **Who died in this story, who killed them, and how did they die?**
   Put in the right names and complete the sentences.

   1 _____ died because he refused to sleep with his wife's
     sister. _____ killed him and hid his body _____.

   2 _____ was just a small-time crook in a world of big tough
     guys – but he died to save his girlfriend. _____ gave him a
     drink which _____.

   3 _____ hadn't killed the pornographer, but the man's lover
     didn't know that. _____ went to his apartment and shot
     him as he _____.

   4 _____ loved the sound of other people's pain, and did the
     dirty work for a man whose own hands remained clean.
     _____ had to kill him to _____.

   5 _____ involved a young woman in pornography – and the
     man who loved her didn't like it. _____ shot him when he
     found him taking _____.

2 **Here is the newspaper report about the deaths of Geiger and**
   Brody, which, as agreed between Marlowe and the police, is
   only partly true (see page 43). Complete the report with the
   right names, and eight of the twelve linking words below.

   (Joe) Brody / (Carol) Lundgren / (Arthur) Geiger
   although / and / and / because / before / but / however / that /
   when / which / who / who

The violent death of _____, a Hollywood bookseller,
has quickly been followed by the death of his killer. The
police report that _____, _____ owned a popular
bookstore on Hollywood Boulevard, was murdered last night
at his home on Laverne Terrace.

_____ the reason for _____'s murder is not known, the
killer, a man called _____, was well known to the police as
a thief. _____ himself, _____, lived for less than twenty
hours after the murder. A young man called _____, _____
worked at _____'s bookstore, went to _____'s
apartment late this afternoon _____ shot him _____ he came to
the door. _____ has now been arrested _____ has told the
police _____ he killed _____ in revenge for the death of his
employer.

3 **Here is the second newspaper report agreed with the police,
about the death of Owen Taylor. Put the parts of sentences in
the right order, and join them to make three sentences.**

1 had recently been ill and unhappy.
2 with Taylor dead at the wheel.
3 A man killed himself last night . . .
4 and the car was later found in the sea . . .
5 Owen Taylor, who worked as a chauffeur for an old
   Hollywood oil family, . . .
6 Yesterday evening he took a Buick . . .
7 by driving into the sea off Lido Pier.
8 which belonged to the family, . . .

4 The police told the newspapers that Owen Taylor killed himself. Was that true? What do you think really happened to him? Was he murdered, and if so, by whom?

5 After Carmen killed Rusty Regan, Vivian asked Eddie Mars for help. Complete her part of their conversation.

VIVIAN: Eddie, you've got to help me! _____

EDDIE: Hey, calm down! What can be so bad? Sit down and let me get you a drink.

VIVIAN: Eddie, listen to me! It's Carmen. She's _____

EDDIE: What do you mean? Who?

VIVIAN: _____

EDDIE: But why would she kill a great guy like Rusty? Where is he? What happened? Was it an accident?

VIVIAN: _____

EDDIE: What? Are you sure? How do you know?

VIVIAN: _____

EDDIE: Hell, Vivian. Things look bad. Does the General know about this?

VIVIAN: _____

EDDIE: Yes, I guess he would. And we must keep them out of this. Does anyone else know what happened?

VIVIAN: _____

EDDIE: Will he keep his mouth shut?

VIVIAN: _____

EDDIE: Good. OK, Vivian. Here's what we'll do. I'll get Mona to help us. I'll send her out of town for a while. There's a place I know . . .

VIVIAN: _____

EDDIE: Don't you see? We'll make people think she ran off with Rusty. It won't be difficult to believe. She's a beautiful girl, my wife. And she'll do anything I say.

VIVIAN: _____

EDDIE: Don't worry, Vivian. I'll think of something you can do for me. Now, come on. Stop crying and fix your face. Get ready to play the cheated wife!

6 **How do you judge these people? Why did they do the things they did? Was what they did right or wrong?**

1 Marlowe killed Canino.
2 Norris kept all the Sternwoods' secrets.
3 Vivian did not tell her father or the police that she knew Carmen had killed Regan.
4 Mona Mars wanted to help Eddie in any way she could.
5 Owen Taylor killed Geiger.
6 Carol Lundgren killed Joe Brody.

7 **Here are some different titles for this story. Which ones do you prefer, and why? Are there any which are not suitable?**

Death in the Sump	Murder in Los Angeles
Death by Cyanide	Marlowe Investigates
Death of a Bootlegger	The Roulette Murders
Death of a Blackmailer	A Cute Blonde
The General's Daughters	The Sternwood Sisters

ABOUT THE AUTHOR

Raymond Chandler was born in Chicago in 1888, but moved to England with his mother when he was twelve. He went to school in London, and later worked as a newspaper reporter and book reviewer. In 1912 he returned to America, and went to live in California. After the First World War, during which he was in the Canadian army, he did a number of different jobs, and then worked for an oil company. He married in 1924.

He did not begin writing fiction until 1933, and his first novel, *The Big Sleep*, appeared in 1939. It was an immediate success. Later novels included *Farewell, My Lovely* (1940), *The High Window* (1942), *The Lady in the Lake* (1943), and *The Long Goodbye* (1953). All these have been made into successful films – the most famous one is probably *The Big Sleep*, made in 1944, starring Humphrey Bogart and Lauren Bacall.

Raymond Chandler is one of the great writers of crime fiction – many people would say the greatest. He believed that style was just as important as the plot, and his writing has been much admired for its clever and amusing use of language. Philip Marlowe, who is almost as well known as Sherlock Holmes, is the first-person narrator of all the novels. He is cool, tough, good-looking, always cracking jokes and never surprised by anything – a hero who stays honest in a hard, dishonest world. In a letter Chandler wrote: 'I see him always in a lonely street, in lonely rooms, puzzled but never quite defeated.'

Like Marlowe, Chandler liked to drink too much. After his wife's death in 1954 his health became poor, and he died in California in 1959.

ABOUT BOOKWORMS

OXFORD BOOKWORMS LIBRARY
Classics • True Stories • Fantasy & Horror • Human Interest
Crime & Mystery • Thriller & Adventure

The OXFORD BOOKWORMS LIBRARY offers a wide range of original and adapted stories, both classic and modern, which take learners from elementary to advanced level through six carefully graded language stages:

Stage 1 (400 headwords)	**Stage 4** (1400 headwords)
Stage 2 (700 headwords)	**Stage 5** (1800 headwords)
Stage 3 (1000 headwords)	**Stage 6** (2500 headwords)

More than fifty titles are also available on cassette, and there are many titles at Stages 1 to 4 which are specially recommended for younger learners. In addition to the introductions and activities in each Bookworm, resource material includes photocopiable test worksheets and Teacher's Handbooks, which contain advice on running a class library and using cassettes, and the answers for the activities in the books.

Several other series are linked to the OXFORD BOOKWORMS LIBRARY. They range from highly illustrated readers for young learners, to playscripts, non-fiction readers, and unsimplified texts for advanced learners.

Oxford Bookworms Starters	*Oxford Bookworms Factfiles*
Oxford Bookworms Playscripts	*Oxford Bookworms Collection*

Details of these series and a full list of all titles in the OXFORD BOOKWORMS LIBRARY can be found in the *Oxford English* catalogues. A selection of titles from the OXFORD BOOKWORMS LIBRARY can be found on the next pages.

BOOKWORMS • CRIME & MYSTERY • STAGE 4

Death of an Englishman

MAGDALEN NABB

Retold by Diane Mowat

It was a very inconvenient time for murder. Florence was full of Christmas shoppers and half the police force was already on holiday.

At first it seemed quite an ordinary murder. Of course, there are always a few mysteries. In this case, the dead man had been in the habit of moving his furniture at three o'clock in the morning. Naturally, the police wanted to know why. The case became more complicated. But all the time, the answer was right under their noses. They just couldn't see it. It was, after all, a very ordinary murder.

BOOKWORMS • CRIME & MYSTERY • STAGE 4

The Hound of the Baskervilles

SIR ARTHUR CONAN DOYLE

Retold by Patrick Nobes

Dartmoor. A wild, wet place in the south-west of England. A place where it is easy to get lost, and to fall into the soft green earth which can pull the strongest man down to his death.

A man is running for his life. Behind him comes an enormous dog – a dog from his worst dreams, a dog from hell. Between him and a terrible death stands only one person – the greatest detective of all time, Sherlock Holmes.

Reflex

DICK FRANCIS

Retold by Rowena Akinyemi

People who ride racehorses love the speed, the excitement, the danger – and winning the race. Philip Nore has been riding for many years and he always wants to win – but sometimes he is told to lose. Why?

And what is the mystery about the photographer, George Millace, who has just died in a car crash?

Philip Nore knows the answer to the first question, and he wants to find out the answer to the second. But as he begins to learn George Millace's secrets, he realizes that his own life is in danger.

The Thirty-Nine Steps

JOHN BUCHAN

Retold by Nick Bullard

'I turned on the light, but there was nobody there. Then I saw something in the corner that made my blood turn cold. Scudder was lying on his back. There was a long knife through his heart, pinning him to the floor.'

Soon Richard Hannay is running for his life across the hills of Scotland. The police are chasing him for a murder he did not do, and another, more dangerous enemy is chasing him as well – the mysterious 'Black Stone'. Who are these people? And why do they want Hannay dead?

BOOKWORMS • FANTASY & HORROR • STAGE 4

The Unquiet Grave

M. R. JAMES

Retold by Peter Hawkins

If you find a locked room in a lonely inn, don't try to open it, even on a bright sunny day. If you find a strange whistle hidden among the stones of an old church, don't blow it. If a mysterious man gives you a piece of paper with strange writing on it, give it back to him at once. And if you call a dead man from his grave, don't expect to sleep peacefully ever again.

Read these five ghost stories by daylight, and make sure your door is locked.

BOOKWORMS • CRIME & MYSTERY • STAGE 5

Deadlock

SARA PARETSKY

Retold by Rowena Akinyemi

V. I. Warshawski, private investigator, Chicago, USA.

People imagine private detectives to be tired-looking men in raincoats, but Vic is female. She's tough, beautiful, carries a gun – and goes on asking questions until she gets answers.

When her cousin Boom Boom dies in an accident, Vic is naturally upset. She wants to know how and why the accident happened, and she isn't satisfied by the answers she gets. So she goes on asking questions . . . and more people start to die.